ALLAN AHLBERG

Slow Dog's Nose

Illustrated by
ANDRÉ AMSTUTZ

VIKING • PUFFIN

VIKING/PUFFIN
Published by the Penguin Group: London, New York, Australia, Canada and New Zealand
Penguin Books Ltd, Registered Offices: Harmondsworth, Middlesex, England

First published by Viking 2000
1 3 5 7 9 10 8 6 4 2
Published in Puffin Books 2000
1 3 5 7 9 10 8 6 4 2

Printed in Hong Kong by Imago Publishing Ltd

A CIP catalogue record for this book is available from the British Library
ISBN 0–670–87995–9 Hardback
ISBN 0–140–56401–2 Paperback

Slow Dog is asleep.
His eyes are asleep.
His ears are asleep.
His mouth and paws and tail are asleep.

But his *nose* is awake.

Sniff, sniff!
Slow Dog sits up and sniffs the air.
Something is cooking.

Then . . . in comes Mother Hen.

"Their window is open!"
yells Mother Hen.
"Their bed is empty!
My chickens have gone!"

Slow Dog helps Mother Hen.

They follow the trail
of the missing chickens.

Sniff, sniff!
What's this?
A little ball.

Sniff, sniff!
What's this?
A little teddy.

Sniff, sniff!
What's this?
A little . . . *feather*.

The trail leads into the woods.
"I . . . smell . . . sausages,"
says Slow Dog.

The trail leads across the field.
"I . . . smell . . . cheeseburgers,"
says Slow Dog.

The trail leads up the hill.
"I . . . smell . . . chickens!"

Oh no!

Oh yes!

Down the hill,
beside the river,
Fast Fox is having
a *barbecue*.

Sausages – yes!
Cheeseburgers – yes!
And . . . chickens –
YES!

Mother Hen
flies down the hill.

Slow Dog falls over . . .
and rolls down it.

The chickens see Mother Hen coming.
"Cheep, cheep!"
Fast Fox sees Mother Hen coming.
"Ha, ha!"

Nobody
sees Slow Dog coming.

Fast Fox grabs Mother Hen.
"Cluck, cluck!"
"Ha, ha!"
"Cheep, cheep!"

Then . . .
down the hill,
out of the green grass
a big slow dog . . .

comes rolling.

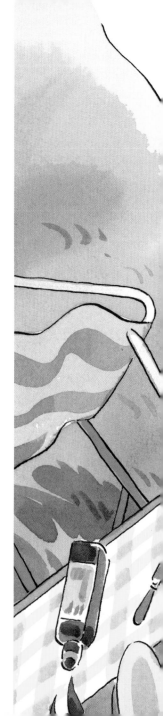

He knocks the table flying.
He knocks the chair flying.
He knocks Fast Fox flying . . .

SPLA

Time goes by.
Slow Dog is asleep again.
His eyes are asleep.
His ears are asleep.
His mouth and paws
and tail are asleep.

But his *nose* is awake.

The End

NOW TURN
OVER

If you liked this story
and you're ready for another
Try

Fast Fox Goes Crazy

In *Fast Fox Goes Crazy*

There is a fox
a bouncy castle
some flying chickens . . .
and a sack!

Oh no!
Those poor little chickens . . .

Who will save them?